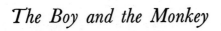

The Boy and the Monkey

LEON GARFIELD

The Boy and the Monkey

Illustrated by

TREVOR RIDLEY

FRANKLIN WATTS, INC.

575 Lexington Avenue

New York, N.Y. 10022

First published 1969
First American publication 1970
by Franklin Watts, Inc.

PRINTED IN GREAT BRITAIN

FOR JANE

I

Come rain, come sun, come doleful November, they trudged the London streets; a sad-eyed boy and his monkey. Tiny creature, scarce bigger than a grown man's fist. Bright in a scarlet jacket, it clung at the boy's brown coat as if it was a second heart . . . and stared out at the passing world with eyes like undertaker's buttons.

How they kept themselves alive was a mystery of the deepest kind. It puzzled the morning milkmaids and the clerks and apprentices as they opened their masters' windows and doors. It puzzled the noonday merchants and gentry, and the tea-time strollers and callers, and the sitters in coffee houses from morning till night.

But most of all it puzzled a lady in Hanover Square one afternoon between four and five o'clock. She came out of a sedan chair with a creak and a rustle and a grand unfolding— like a black furry cabbage blooming in the dusk. Paid off the chairmen and was about to enter her mansion. Then she saw the boy and his monkey standing in the gloom. They were the saddest objects she'd ever seen in her comfortable life. She shivered and drew her furs about her.

"How do they keep body and soul together?" she whispered to herself.

The boy's large ears, flattened under his shabby hat, were sharp as knives.

"Gawd knows," he answered truthfully; but didn't mention

that there were others who knew, too . . . and maybe wouldn't have been so tolerant if ever they'd laid hands on him.

The lady sighed and fumbled in her purse.

"I ain't a beggar, ma'am," said the boy proudly. "I ain't come to that, yet."

The lady's great sentimental heart boomed inside her. The boy's eyes grew enormous with hopeful gloom.

"Then what—?" murmured the lady.

"I aim to sell me little friend," said the boy with a somewhat rusty catch in his voice. "Me monkey, here. Got to keep from starvin' some'ow."

The lady was taken aback; but, being already set on charity, there was no stopping her.

"Is it—is he a clean monkey? Is he a quiet, gentle monkey, child? He don't tear furnishings or scratch servants?"

"Oh no, ma'am! He's a real genteel monkey. Well brought on. Name of Pistol—"

"Very well," said the lady, affecting all the sternness of the tender-hearted. "I'll buy your monkey for five pound. Just so you can keep yourself alive, child."

She counted out the money and put it in the boy's trembling hand. Then she took the monkey's brass chain. Obligingly, Pistol hopped onto her arm and peered enviously into her furs. They were so much more handsome than its own, which was gray as dust. Then it sat upright as it was carried off into its grand new home . . . while its one-time friend and master went his ways, looking sadder than ever in spite of the five pounds.

An hour later, when the rich square was sunk into shadows, the boy came mournfully back and stopped before the mansion in which his monkey now lived. Like a ghost he stood there, haunting the place of his loss.

He glanced up and down the street. No one came. He looked up to the windows, then to the roof. He began to whistle . . .

Something stirred, high up. A scrap of scarlet lipped the chimney pot like a blown spark. Then it vanished. Now a tiny shadow moved neat and quick down the mansion's unsuspecting face. Now it was gone. And so was the boy.

Once more they trudged the cold November streets, the sad-eyed boy and his monkey . . .

"What 'ave you got for me this time, Pistol?" muttered the boy, whose name was Tim—though who'd given it him was lost somewhere near the beginning of his eleven years. There was much about Tim that was gone beyond knowing. Though he'd begun life as a foundling, he was now more like a lostling . . . "Well, Pistol—let's 'ave it."

The monkey held out a silver spoon and a salt-cellar. Tim sniffed and pocketed them, muttering the while:

"Oh Pistol! You're nought but a common thief and will be 'anged! But that ain't the worst of it! You ain't got no sense. I'd 'ave thought your masters before me would 'ave taught you all what glitters ain't gold. Seven shilling at most is all we'll get for today's silver. We'll be greybeards afore we're prosperous at this rate!"

Tim was exactly right. Seven shillings to the penny he got from a gent in St Anne's Court. The monkey watched dismally as the pretty spoon and salt-cellar were changed into worn coins. Would he never please its master? Would it never get whatever it was its mysterious monkey heart desired?

Two masters had it known already. The first had been the piratical sailor who'd plucked it, a wrinkled baby, from the forests of Brazil to crouch upon his slippery shoulder through many a wicked northward mile till they'd come to Virginia, and thence to Gravesend in that year of no grace at all, 1740. The second had been a cruel fat highwayman who'd given it its name then passed it on complete, so to speak, to Tim in exchange for an errand.

Indeed, Pistol had seen much of the world, and none of it wonderfully honest. Even Tim, the third master, on whom all the monkey's unknown hopes were pinned, could hardly be relied on. The last cherry-stone on the plate was Tim—neither rich man . . . poor man . . . beggar man, but thief.

Nonetheless, there was great fondness between the monkey and the boy. Each was the other's only companion and friend. At the end of the day they would return to their lodgings above a tavern in Poland Street, where they would dine off the best their money could buy. If food was what kept body and soul together, then Tim's were in no great danger of being parted. When they'd done eating, Tim would chatter to Pistol of his hopes and dreams; and Pistol would blink and stare at this third master whom it loved best of all and yet who could see no further into its monkey heart than the pirate or the highwayman before him.

"Five pound seven shillings," said Tim sleepily. "We'll 'ave to do better than that if we wants to retire an' be law-abiding, Pistol. If we goes on like this, we'll be felons all our lives . . . But maybe tomorrow, eh?"

The next morning was dull and yellowish and threatening fog. A poor beginning. The weather needed to be sharp and clear for Tim's melancholy face to make its best effect. He might stretch it as long as a boot, but it would touch no one if not seen; and though, in his day, he'd wrung more hearts than an Aldgate washerwoman sheets, he'd never done well in the fog. So it was with no great hopes that the boy and the monkey trudged to Half Moon Street, off Piccadilly, to watch the crested carriages come and go.

Thus it happened that he looked more than ordinarily dismal; and, catching a sight of himself in a carriage window, he breathed admiringly:

"Gawd, Pistol! I'd almost give meself a guinea to cheer meself up!"

But stony hearts passed him by and passed him by, till half after twelve when—he heard a high, clear voice demanding:

"Mr Perry! That urchin with the monkey. Ask him why he stands there so—so aggravatingly."

"A bite, a bite! Oh Pistol! We got a bite!"

The lady who spoke was young, handsome and had every right to look pleased with herself. She sat in a crested (though old-fashioned) carriage with a rosy rich admirer. On her finger—displayed at the window sill—was a diamond that would have purchased the Prince of Wales.

"Lovebirds, Pistol! An' I think we've netted 'em!"

"Well, Mr Perry—jump to it, sir! Remember, I'm still Lady Margaret—not Mrs Perry yet."

She laughed; a merry, tinkling sound, like a dish full of shillings.

Mr Perry undid his eyes from the diamond.

"Your lightest wish, my love, is my command." He laughed also—but more breathily. "Haven't I already plucked down a star for your finger? Ha—ha!"

"You boasting, vulgar merchant, you! Now—go along and do my bidding, sir! I command."

"A right pair we got 'ere, Pistol! But watch it! They can't be as simple as they look. Not 'im, anyways."

Mr Perry, in blue coat and lavender breeches, jumped lightly down from the carriage.

"Boy! What are you about eh?"

The boy with the monkey on his shoulder shuffled a few paces nearer; bent his head as if he was hard of hearing, in addition to all his other misfortunes.

"Ask him—ask him how he keeps body and soul together,

Mr Perry. I take an interest in the poor, y'know."

"Well, boy; tell us how it's done, eh?"

"Dunno," said Tim. "But I ain't a beggar. I ain't come to that, yet. I—I'm 'ere to sell me little friend. 'unger 'as driven me to it. 'unger an' misery, sir. But I still got me pride."

"Buy it, Mr Perry. My wish."

"What?"

"The—the monkey. Come sir—your word!"

"But—"

"The boy has pride. 'Tis to be respected. Always respect pride, Mr Perry. This you must learn, sir, before you marry me."

Mr Perry's rosy face went a shade rosier. "Your lightest wish."

Tim endeavored to look proud. But at the same time he tried to suggest that, had they been more equal, he'd have been glad to wink at Mr Perry. Perhaps he *did* wink at him, for Mr Perry's smile grew suddenly cold. His eyes glinted, and under his loving softness there peeped out the hard, ruthless spirit that had kept him one of the richest merchants in the City.

"Here's ten pound, boy. Now—give me the monkey and be off!"

The fog lay up in the sky till after three o'clock. Then it came sweeping down. It came in huge yellow bolsters that swallowed up streets and lanes and mansions and parks and the great wide river itself, so the faint voices of watermen crying their fares, came eerily from a nowhere that gurgled and lapped.

Now currents in the air began to twist the vapors between the invisible buildings, making of emptiness another town, with domes and spires and sudden dark doorways that swirled and dissolved into yellow nothingness.

Feet shuffled, sticks tapped and, here and there, a dream horse neighed in alarm. Then, maybe, a ghostly coachman would comfort it with, "Easy . . . easy, m'dear. You ain't on the moon, but down 'ere in Piccadilly—or Dover Street . . . or even Whitechapel, for all I knows . . . And—and that ain't a goblin but . . . well—it might 'ave been a mortal boy—"

The mournful shape of what might have been a mortal boy trudged along what could have been Half Moon Street and vanished into the thick, yellow air. Only the sound of his feet was heard; then there was silence.

Suddenly there came a sound of whistling. A strange, piercing melody that went through the fog like an arrow. It continued for a full five minutes, and caused much wondering and un-easiness in the neighborhood.

Then it stopped and was heard no more. A moment later, the coachman with the restless horse saw again the vague shape of what might have been a mortal boy trudge by. And nestling at his chest, no bigger than a grown man's fist, was something that could have been—might quite possibly have been—a monkey . . .

Along Piccadilly the fog was horribly thick. There was no prospect of finding Poland Street. But toward Haymarket, the air turned briefly threadbare and went into holes. Through one of these holes, Tim and Pistol spied the Saracen's Head— a small, obscure tavern that lurked between two houses as if it had been arrested while trying to make off.

The painted sign smiled a Turkish welcome; but as the boy and his monkey passed beneath, this same smile seemed sud-

denly to grow cruel. Narrow painted eyes peered ominously down and the board swung and creaked like a gibbet.

Yet within, there was such a press of respectable gentlemen taking refuge from the fog that all uneasiness sank away.

"What 'ave you got for me this time, Pistol, you 'orrible little thief?" whispered Tim, affectionately, when they'd found a corner.

The monkey blinked its withered lids. Then, with an expression of piteous hope, it held out its skinny hand. Had it done right this time? Was its dream about to come true? Was this third master the one who'd grant its mysterious wish? For—it had stolen the diamond! Lady Margaret's ring!

Of a sudden, the babble of voices in the smoky parlor seemed like a great Hallelujah Chorus, crashing the roof and taking Tim up into a heaven of liveried footmen, a carriage and a house in a square. There was nothing he could not buy with such riches!

"Oh you sweet beast, you!" he breathed, his eyes brimming with real tears. "You shall 'ave dainty nuts from the Indies, grapes an' rare fruits from wonderful 'ot lands across the seas! You shall sleep in a little gilded bed with 'olland drapes and downy pillers to ease your darlin' 'ead!"

But whatever hope it was that burned in the monkey's breast, nuts and grapes and soft pillows seemed to be no part of it. Its tiny face crumpled and it began to chatter in a bitter rage.

Bewildered, Tim stared at his little friend. How had he offended? What was wrong? He reached out—

The monkey hopped back—its face wild and wretched. "Pistol!"

Curious faces turned; began to smile, chuckle . . . A humorous gentlemen with dark red cheeks, pursed his lips and whistled at the monkey. Directly, the sound was taken up and the parlor was suddenly filled with knives and pins and bodkins of noise.

Terrified, Pistol began to dart about—

"Fer pity's sake, gents!" cried the boy. "Give over! 'E'll go mad! 'E'll fly off an' be lost! Pistol—Pistol! Fer Pity's sake—"

But there was no stopping the parlour's amusement in the sight of the dismal urchin plunging and stumbling after his scarlet-jacketed monkey. They whistled and whistled with lips like a field of poppies.

The din grew formidable. Faster and faster hopped the tormented Pistol; while every now and then the light touched on something that sparked and winked so the creature seemed to have hold of a fistful of fire. And Tim, no less in anguish, blundered a yard behind, tripping over feet, stools and sticks—

"Pistol—Gents, *please* . . ."

Now it leaped on shoulders and wigs, even mounting up the stairways of powdered curls—

"Pistol! Come back to me! Oh—oh! My Gawd! We're done for! It's 'im!"

Tim's knees fell a-trembling. His teeth began to chatter. His face grew white and his heart dropped so far and fast that, had he not been wearing good boots, it would surely have gone through the floor.

Pistol had hopped on a fatal shoulder, and plucked at a terrible wig! An iron shoulder in blue velvet cloth.

Mr Perry's face was staring into Tim's! Mr Perry, who'd likewise taken refuge from the fog.

His smooth, rosy countenance seemed to blaze in Tim's

sky like a savage sun. On which Pistol, as if for some vengeful purpose deep in its monkeyish soul, did a fearful thing. It held out its hand and gave its wretched master the stolen diamond ring.

"You are a thief!" said Mr Perry, harshly. "And will be hanged. There is no escape. I have a hundred witnesses."

The uproar in the parlor died away. Everyone stared at the boy. They marked him well, so there should be no mistake when they should be called to swear his life away. And in the silence, there could be heard quite clearly the painted sign outside, swinging on its hinges and sounding more like a gibbet than ever. Truly, Tim and Pistol never had much luck in the fog.

II

Tuesday, December 3rd and a fine rain falling. It prickled the river and rinsed the streets and lanes and the jumbled rooftops. It made clean pathways down the faces of early morning urchins and even washed the dreadful frontage of Newgate Gaol and the Sessions House beside it . . . as if in preparation.

Through this cold, piercing rain, hastening from Black-friars, Shoreditch, Holborn and Cheapside, came twelve good men and true—all in their funeral best. One by one, they entered the Sessions House, where Tim's trial was to take place, peevish with damp and steaming gently as the warm, offensive air smote them through and through and through. Their feet clumped on the wooden boards like grumbling thunder.

"The jury's come," grunted a turnkey to the dismal gathering of thieves and vagabonds in a stone chamber below the court.

Whereupon, watched by doleful eyes, he mounted the thirteen stairs to a doorway. He peeped and listened, and held up his hand for silence below.

"They're being sworn," he murmured, as he watched the twelve men. "He-he! To render true an' honest verdicts on all of you wicked gents. There's a pair of carpenters; a bricklayer; three drapers; a vintner; a silversmith; an innkeeper (bless him!); an' three gents in marine stores from Pudding Lane. Twelve good men an' true, as they say."

He grinned, and was obliged with a mumble that passed for laughter. He shrugged his shoulders. After all, he was only trying to cheer up the unlucky souls who waited to be judged.

Truly, they were a miserable lot. Only a foxy-faced baronet's son who'd been declaring since early morning that no judge or jury would dare to convict *him*, looked reasonably happy. The rest looked glum as sin and most glum of all the boy and his monkey who'd stolen Lady Margaret's famous diamond ring.

"Cheer up, Tim!" the turnkey said amiably. "It ain't the end of the world, lad!" Then he bit his lip when he realized that, for Tim, it most likely was. So he added, "Yet," and went back to eavesdrop on the court.

"Oh Pistol!" whispered Tim, near fainting from the confined prison stink that no vinegar, pomander nor herbs could sweeten, "We're goners now! All our 'opes an' dreams must come to nought on Tyburn Tree!"

He sighed, and for once the gloom on his face went as deep as his soul. His brief life passed unhappily before him; and there were tears in his eyes when he wondered what would become of Pistol when he was gone.

While he was so engaged, the turnkey, meaning for the best, explained that the court was filling up and that the jury had gone off to choose their foreman and that his money was on the innkeeper, "a real, natural-born leader of men."

He was right. The innkeeper—a tremendous fellow with a face like pewter—was chosen.

"I take it, gents," he said, peeping about him as if for signs

of rebellion, "that we're none of us weak-livered about the hanging of proper felons? I take it we're all ready and willing to do our duty and send them what deserves it to Tyburn? I take it we're none of us feeble-minded enough to be plagued by bad dreams on what reely ain't any of our business? Right, gents? Agreed? Them what's guilty gets the chop. And the Lord have mercy on their souls: male, female, old or young."

There were no signs of rebellion. The foreman nodded and the twelve good men and true went back into the court for their day of judgement where once more the turnkey could observe them and report on their doings to his anxious charges below.

"He's coming!" said the turnkey, of a sudden; and a shudder went through the ragged limbs of the accused. Pale faces went paler yet, and souls which never till then had had a religious twinge, thought directly upon God. It was ten o'clock and the judge had arrived.

Lord Coke: a stern, bent old man whose shriveled face sat in the midst of his great wig giving him the appearance of a villainous old sheep. He glanced sourly around the court; then he looked contemptuously at the foreman of the jury as if to say, "I want no nonsense from you, sir. Just bring in the verdict as I bid, and we'll get through the day somehow."

But the foreman, who was a natural-born leader of men and proud of it, returned the judge's look with interest. "You can talk till your ears fly off, m'lud," his large face seemed to say. "It won't make a dram of difference. We'll bring in a verdict as *we* see fit. *And* we'll get through the day somehow—even if it takes all night!"

"There's going to be trouble," murmured the sharp-eyed turnkey.

It was perfectly plain that the foreman and the judge both thought the other an obstinate old fool. Consequently, each set out with no more lofty aim than to take the other down all the pegs he could. But cautiously.

His Lordship knew full well that, if he betrayed any inclination in his summing up, the great oaf of a foreman would bully the jurors into bringing in an opposite verdict. Just to spite him. So Lord Coke had to dust up his wits and polish his brain in order to present summings-up of extraordinary fairness.

So the innkeeper-foreman, as each prisoner was brought up from below to stand his trial, was unable to decide what the haughty judge would have liked the verdict to be. He had no choice but to let his eleven good men and true vote according to their own consciences. He'd turn to them each time with a puzzled but honest, "What's your pleasure this time, gen'lemen?"

Verdicts came in that astonished everyone by their justice; and learned attorneys found themselves quite put out by a judge who seemed to be on nobody's side.

Gentlemen were convicted and beggars were freed, with no regard to anything but the evidence. Even the baronet's son who went up the thirteen stairs with a proud sneer on his face and a witty speech on his lips was whisked in and out of the dock with no regard at all to his hopes and expectations.

His father had spoken with an uncle who'd talked to a friend
who'd mentioned it to a debtor who'd written to a duchess

who'd whispered it—over coffee—to Lord Coke himself. The
young man had counted much on this chain of salvation;
but his lordship appeared as indifferent to it as if he'd been the
blind goddess of justice herself. Duchess or no, he could not
afford to betray himself to the foreman who watched him like
a portly hawk.

"And what's your pleasure this time, gen'lemen?"

"Guilty . . . guilty . . . guilty . . ."

So the baronet's son went his ways as briefly and justly as did
the rest of the day's accused. His witty speech died on his lips
and his elegant gesture sank to a tremble. The audience in the

courtroom who'd leaned forward, fell back disappointed—as if a favored actor had been replaced by an understudy who'd not been up to his part.

"It's your turn now, lad," said the turnkey to Tim.

"We're goners, ain't we," sighed the boy, mounting the fateful stairs. "We're done for, mister . . . an' that's a fact."

The turnkey nodded. Tim was right. But he was so moved —as much by Pistol as by Tim—that he smiled kindly and said, meaning for the best; "Cheer up, lad! Better luck next time!" Then he bit his lip when he realized that, for Tim, there would be no next time.

He sniffed and opened the door into the dock, and Tim and
Pistol climbed the last step and went into the iron jaws of the
court. So tragic was their aspect that it would have melted
a heart of stone. Unhappily, there were no such hearts to greet
them; only the cold dislike of the judge and the foreman of the
jury for each other.

They trudged into their place and up to the rusty spikes
that guarded the dock as if it was but a brief halting place—a
station—on a journey that was nearing its end.

"Leastways, we got a good crowd," whispered Tim, to give
his monkey courage. But Pistol crouched in the hollow of Tim's
neck, with thin arms outstretched as if to defend them both
against the hangman. And from this pale and grubby refuge,
it stared out at the crowded court.

Its tiny face was terrible with something like remorse. Its
wrinkled lids lay across its black eyes as if all the sins of the
world were weighing them down; yet they would not shut.
Not all the sins of the world were heavy enough to curtain off

this remorse. It must needs look and look and grieve in its monkey's heart for such things as only a monkey can know.

Its look struck a chill through the court, and it was in vain for someone to whisper, "They always look sad." No monkey had ever looked so sad as this one.

"Never mind, Pistol," muttered Tim, feeling his friend's heart fairly popping with fear. "They won't 'ang you. Not a poor, ignorant beast. Most likely, you'll go to Mister Ketch, the 'angman. For there ain't much else about me 'e'll want. So you'll end up a law-abiding monkey, after all."

Now the charge was read and the witnesses called: five respectable gentlemen, and the landlord of the Saracen's Head, who had all seen the monkey hand the ring to Tim. Then Lady Margaret gave her evidence in her high clear voice. Told how Mr Perry had bought her the monkey; told of the loss of the ring. And Mr Perry identified the ring as the very one he'd purchased and given that day to the lady.

As he handled it, the diamond flashed and glittered and seemed to burn. It drew all eyes as it was passed from hand to hand by the jury. It seemed to dance, almost, from palm to palm like a firefly. Here, it loitered; there, it sprang . . . and a hand seemed to go after it, as if to snare it back.

Even the stern judge grew absorbed in its passage; and Mr Perry watched it with a proud, indulgent eye. None had thought any more for Tim and Pistol, who eyed the jewel with anything but affection.

"You was right, Pistol. We should 'ave stuck to silver. We never was very lucky in the fog . . ."

Now the diamond was in the foreman's stubby hand. His heavy, pewterish face was bent down, observing the beauty of the jewel that was to bring the child in the dock to the gallows. Feeling many eyes upon him, he looked up. He caught the monkey's gaze. Large as he was, he shrank before it. His heart ached; his eyes watered; his hand shook . . . .

"Psst! Psst!"

A lowly juryman was leaning forward to catch his attention. It was the silversmith. Wrinkled little man with a pair of chipped pink eyes. A well-known authority on jewels. He would have another look at the diamond. The foreman passed it back.

The silversmith held it up to the light; then weighed it in his hand; then put it to his mouth as if to kiss it. Cold embrace! Now he pursed his lips and sighed:

"Matchless! I never saw one so 'andsome, clean an' white. 'Tis a miracle of nature—a masterpiece of God!"

In the well of the court, Mr Perry looked grand and proud— and Lady Margaret flushed under the diamond's icy flattery of her worth.

Lord Coke, remembering the horrible foreman, fixed his eyes on nothing in particular.

"Prisoner at the bar," he said, avoiding the monkey's gaze lest compassion should weaken his decision, "you stand accused of privately stealing, from the house of Lady Margaret Howard, the ring that is before this court. What have you to say in your defense?"

Mournfully, Tim looked at the stern judge, the stern jury, the stern court—whose very walls and windows seemed to have been designed for the sole purpose of frowning on him. It was a stern world, in which he felt a trespasser. "Be off out of it!" everyone and everything seemed to be saying; and the way out for him would be the hangman's rope.

"Have you anything to say?" repeated the judge.

Tim shook his head. "Nuffink . . . nuffink . . ."

With face of stone and voice to match, Lord Coke summed up. Neither spite nor mercy nor compassion nor contempt affected him. It was a day of justice. In clear terms the evidence was recalled. Plain and unvarnished. And it was damning. Nonetheless, as was his duty, the judge reminded the jury that the accused was innocent until proven guilty. And the burden of such proof lay with them. There, he stopped. His duty was done. The responsibility was now upon the jury. He gave them leave to consider their verdict. The good men and true shuffled off out of the court into the dismal little room set aside for them.

"When I'm gone, Pistol," mumbled Tim, "I'll come back an' 'awnt your new master. An' maybe then I'll be able to tell 'im whatever it is your 'eart desires, and whatever it is what'll make you smile . . . "

In the juryroom, the twelve men sat round the long table—much scarred and blotted with previous juries' thoughts and problems—and looked to their foreman to ask what was their pleasure.

But for once, the foreman was silent. The memory of the tragical monkey lingered in his heart. It reminded him of things he'd long since forgotten . . . of all the sadnesses he'd seen in his life, by roadsides, in corners and in stone doorways.

What would become of the monkey when its master was hanged? Would its heart break and would it pine and die? Most likely.

The foreman sniffed and rubbed his nose. He tried to guess if the judge had intended any compassion in his summing up. If so, he, the foreman, would have been happy to oblige. But the judge had betrayed nothing. Only the evidence. The weight was upon the jury.

Miserably the foreman looked about him. For the first time the heaviness of his task sat like a lump of lead on his heart.

"What's your—your pleasure this time, gen'lemen?" he

muttered. "If such a dooty can be aught but a disaster and a dismay?"

The jurymen looked to one another. Here was a clear direction to mercy. No doubt of it. But how? How, in the face of the evidence could they do anything but find the wretched child, "Guilty . . . guilty . . . guilty . . . ," and let his monkey die of a broken heart?

"If such a dooty can be aught but a souring of sweet wine and a curdling of souls?"

The jurymen looked down at the battered table. Others before them had had like problems—and had voted as they did now.

"Guilty . . . guilty . . . guilty . . . "

For how could they ignore the evidence without striking at

the goddess of justice herself? The poor, skinny monkey had no choice but to die.

"Guilty . . . guilty . . . guilty . . . ," and let the hangman have the monkey for his own.

The foreman sniffed again. "If such a dooty can be aught but a serving of short measure and a disgrace to him what serves it?"

The last of the jurymen shook their heads, disgraced in spite of themselves.

"Guilty . . . guilty . . ."

"Guilty," muttered the foreman, casting the last vote. "Now, gen'lemen, for the value of this piece of private stealing."

He stared bleakly at the silversmith whose task it was to state the value of the ring. Of a sudden, the silversmith felt like the hangman. His was to be the last voice in the long chain. The foreman continued to stare at him. "It's the law, mister. Remember the law."

Eleven pairs of eyes were upon the silversmith; and in his heart, a twelfth pair—the sad black eyes of the monkey.

"The law, mister. Remember the law."

His chipped old eyes, which were dim with tears, suddenly seemed to brighten. He had remembered the law.

"Bear up, young 'un!" whispered the turnkey from his doorway as he saw the boy and his monkey droop as if to fall. "The jury's come back. It won't be long now. It's almost over." Then once more he bit his injured lip when he realized that what was almost over was Tim's life.

Lord Coke turned to the jury.

"Have you reached a verdict?"

"We have, m'lord," answered the foreman.

"And that verdict is?"

"Guilty, my lord," said the foreman heavily.

"And that is the verdict of you all?"

"It is."

"Prisoner at the bar," said Lord Coke, striving to keep the sadness out of his voice. "You have been found guilty of privately stealing, from Lady Margaret Howard, a ring worth—" Here, he turned to the foreman again. "Worth what? You must say. It is the law. Have you decided?"

"We have, my lord."

The court shifted forward. They had been waiting for this moment. The purchase of the diamond had been famous. Many of Mr Perry's rivals and Lady Margaret's friends were present. There had been much guessing as to how much Mr Perry had been able to afford for the luxury of a noble wife. How much was Lady Margaret worth?

"Elevenpence halfpenny," said the foreman uneasily, and rapidly sat down.

"*What?*"

"Elevenpence halfpenny, my lord."

Astonished, the judge stared at the foreman. And the foreman stared at the judge. It was impossible to tell what each thought of the other. Then the suspicion, the very faintest suspicion of a twitch caught at the corners of the judge's mouth.

"Very well," he murmured. "*Very* well. Prisoner at the bar,

42

you have been found guilty of privately stealing a ring worth—
um—elevenpence halfpenny. Ha-ha! Hm! Elevenpence halfpenny. I must tell you," he went on severely, "that had the
jury decided that it had been worth so much as a penny more,
you would have been hanged. That is the law. But—but the
jury in their wisdom, have valued the ring at . . . ha-ha! at
elevenpence halfpenny. And I must say—"

But whatever it was that the judge had had to say, was lost,
quite drowned out under a sudden storm of shouts, cries and
uproarious laughter from the amazed court.

Mr Perry, regardless of where he was, was shaking his fist at the learned judge; and Lady Margaret, scarlet with shame, was endeavoring to escape from the horrible court.

"A re-trial! A re-trial!" shrieked Mr Perry. "There was prejudice! The jury was bribed! The court's corrupt! I demand a re-trial!"

Then his voice, too, sank under the waves of helpless laughter and roars of, "Elevenpence halfpenny!"

At last order was partly restored and the judge could once more be heard. He spoke, not to the prisoner—who was in a state of startled collapse and was being revived by the cheerful turnkey—but to the raging Mr Perry.

"Do you set your pride above a child's life, sir? Would you have his neck broke so you can hold your head high?"

In mid-fury, Mr Perry stopped. He looked about him- -at his sneering rivals, at the grinning court (whose very windows seemed to chuckle), at the furious lady he'd just lost, and then at the dock where the tiny monkey clung to the bars and stared at the court in bewilderment.

Mr Perry said haltingly, "I—I apologize, my lord. You are—are right. The ring has been truly valued. Very truly."

The smiles died. The judge nodded. Lady Margaret stared hard at the proud merchant who had now admitted, in open court, that his own pride and her value were not above elevenpence halfpenny.

Then she, too, looked about her—from judge to jury to curious, expectant court—and to Pistol in the dock. Beside the monkey now, palely rising on the amiable turnkey's arm, was the accused child. And upon a table, she saw her diamond, still winking and blazing with its own glory. Then she understood what Mr Perry had seen. She said,

"Likewise with Mr Perry, my lord, I agree with the jury. The stone is worth no more than the court has declared. For so long as a child's life is valued at a shilling, then the hugest diamond in the world can be worth no more than elevenpence halfpenny. To value it above would be a mockery of justice and a shame to us all. But—but Mr Perry, sir, no matter what its value, the trinket still pleases me. I'll be honored to wear it again as your betrothal gift, sir . . . "

She fell silent. Then she and Mr Perry resumed their seats.

Her hand was on his arm, and it was plain there was a tenderness between them that was as strong as it was sudden and new.

The judge caught himself smiling. Abruptly, he remembered who he was, and where he was. The heavy foreman of the jury was still watching him like a fat pewter hawk. Lord Coke scowled. Much as he would have liked to be merciful and kindly, and send the wretched urchin and his monkey packing with no worse than a warning, he knew it was impossible. He was there to pass sentence. That was the law. There was no way out. He frowned and frowned and screwed up his features so that his small, shriveled face in his great wig looked more and more like a savage old sheep.

Tim groaned: "Now for it, Pistol, ole friend. Though 'e can't 'ang us, 'e'll do the next worse thing!"

"Prisoner at the bar; though you may not be hanged for your crime, you must still be punished. It is my painful duty to sentence you to be transported, for not less than seven years, to His Majesty's Colony in Virginia, where your bond will be purchased and you will work as your purchaser directs. For seven years. In Virginia."

"Could have been worse," mumbled the turnkey. "He could have made it fourteen. So cheer up, lad. Think of it as a 'oliday!"

Tim sighed. He looked at the judge. Lord Coke, his duty done, permitted himself a gentle smile. The lad and his monkey were a touching pair. Had they been in the street, the judge might well have given them a guinea . . . or even bought the monkey.

46

From force of habit, Tim looked sad again. But within, he was quite hopeful.

"We ain't lost our touch, Pistol. Did you see the sour old justice on the melt? Oh yes, me darlin'! Wherever there's 'earts, in London, on ship or in faraway Virginia, I fancy, you an' me will always be able to melt 'em!"

Affectionately he turned to gaze in his friend's marvelously miserable face. But what had happened? Where were those undertaker's eyes? They were twinkling! If ever a monkey grinned, it was Pistol!

"What's up?" breathed Tim. "'Ave you got your 'eart's

desire? Oh Pistol! You *'ave!* An' to think—I might 'ave been 'anged! You 'orrible little thief, you!"

Pistol, the monkey grinned and grinned into its third master's shining face. Its wish had been granted, its dream come true. Third time lucky indeed. At last, at long last, it was on its way to its warm and comfortable home. By way of Virginia. The first step was achieved. What it had managed once, it could surely manage again. From Virginia to Brazil was but a tiny hop to such as Pistol. This third master was so very kind and obliging.